# *Richard Scarry's* Find Your A B C's

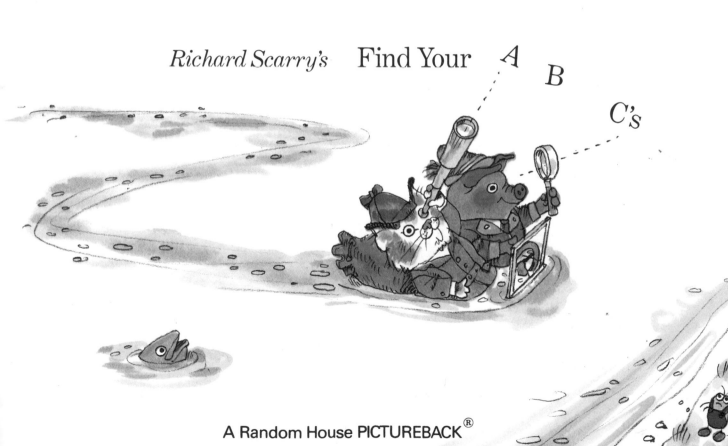

A Random House PICTUREBACK®

# Richard Scarry's

# FIND YOUR

# ABC's

Random House 🏠 New York

Copyright © 1973 by Richard Scarry. All rights reserved under International and Pan-American Copyright Conventions. Published in the United States by Random House, Inc., New York, and simultaneously in Canada by Random House of Canada Limited, Toronto. *Library of Congress Cataloging-in-Publication Data:* Scarry, Richard. Richard Scarry's find your ABC's. (A Random House pictureback) Originally published: Find your ABC's. New York: Random House, 1973. SUMMARY: With the help of the reader, two detectives search for the letters of the alphabet. [1. Mystery and detective stories. 2. Animals—Fiction. 3. Alphabet] I. Title. II. Title: Find your ABC's.   PZ7.S327Rkf   1986   [E]   86-447   ISBN: 0-394-82683-3   Manufactured in the United States of America

This is Sam.    This is Dudley.

They are two very fine detectives.
Sam and Dudley can find almost anything.
Sometimes they fix themselves up so nobody
will recognize them. They wear disguises.

Look at that sack of potatoes.
Would you think it was a detective
looking for something?
    No! Of course not.
    But it is.
    That sack of potatoes is SAM,
in disguise!

And who is this lady
putting on lipstick?
Would you believe that it
isn't a lady at all?
It's Dudley, in *his* disguise!

But what are Sam and Dudley looking for now?
They are looking for all the letters
in the alphabet. Will YOU help them?

As you read this book you will find
that many objects and characters have
their name printed near them. On each
page one letter of the alphabet is
featured in these names.
    *Almost* always it is printed in red.
These red letters are easy to find.
    But on the same page the same letter of
the alphabet is printed *twice* in black.
Once it is a capital letter. The other
time it is a small letter.
    Why not put on *your* disguise and help
Sam and Dudley hunt for all these letters.
    On the last page, you will find out what
Sam and Dudley do with them.

# A a

artist

painting

oak

pan

antenna

ax

can

apples

pail

grass

hat

glasses

Sam and Dudley have disguised themselves
as Indians on horseback. Look at all
the red letters they have found. Wow!

arrow

an
angry
ant

tractor

splash

road

weather vane

balloon

Alfred Alligator,

tail

aviator

barn

airplane

falling leaf

laundry

feather

cabbage patch

wagon

rake

But can you help them find the two
"A's" that are in black? One is a big "A."
The other is a small "a." After you have
found them, put them in Sam's sack,
then turn the page and look for
the next letters.

# B b

bird

bell

broom

Captain Bob

blue boat

BARBER

BAKERY

buildings

Albert Bug

bunny baby

ball

BEWARE

boy

buoy

Sam and Dudley have driven to the harbor.
Dudley forgot to step on the brake!
Look where they have landed!

They will have trouble finding a
big black "B" and a little black "b"
while they are in the water.

Can YOU find them?

box

# C c

cone

raccoon

cap

church

clock

Captain Crocodile

cane

canoe

Look at that crazy accident!
A cat's coat is going to be covered
with ketchup.

cherries

cucumber

corn

carrot

ketchup

grocer

crate

crane

GROCERIES

Put your big "C" and little "c"
into Sam's wet sack, and let's go on.

# D d

a delicious hot dog with mustard

HOT DOGS

Drink Lemonade!

door

Sam and Dudley have driven down to the sandy beach. Detective Sam has found all the red "D's," but he can't find the black ones. Where are they hiding?

Daddy

sand

doll

daisy

diaper

derrick

dump truck

Tillie, the deep-water diver

Doctor Dog bandaging a head

bandage

head

hot dog

M.D.

# E e

elm tree

Edward Leopard,
a very excited
life saver

umbrella

shower

TOILETS
← ENTER
HERE

reel

dressing rooms

eyeglasses

needles

thread

Father sleeping

seashell

shovel

And where is Detective Dudley?
Is he in a dressing room?
I don't think so.
He must be looking for "E's."
   Try to find Dudley
and all the "E's."

eleven sand fleas fleeing

waves

elephant

speedboat

submarine

# F f

forest

fence

Freddy Fox

flag

Farmer Alfalfa

A fire has broken out at Farmer Alfalfa's farm.
Five firemen have come to put it out.
In the river a funny frog is looking for "F's."

a flaming
football

five
firemen

fire engine

fruit

Fresh Fruit a

fisherman

funny
frog

ferryboat

four fish

# G g

Goodness gracious!
Grandma's wagon got knocked over.
Dudley is looking for "G's." Have *you*
found any? When you have found Dudley and
all the "G's," Sam has a good riddle for you.

grapes

glasses

Grandma Pig

wagon

GOODIES
GROWN IN
GRANDMA'S
GARDEN

Gertie
Goose

engine

awning

a young
girl goat

eggs

Vegetables

big
jug

bag

green grass

bridge

garbage can

Here is Sam's good riddle:
What has two feet and flies?
Do you know the answer? Do you give up?
Well, the answer is—
Dudley, disguised as a garbage can!

# H h

Tillie and Miss Honey, the schoolteacher,
are having a lawn party for the children.
Hear the orchestra happily playing.
But Sam is high in the air, about to hit
the shortcake.
Can he be gathering "H's"?

Tillie

Miss Honey

*Heavens!*

*Horrors!*

heel

hat

head

Henny Hen

harp

Harry
Heron

horn

harmonica

Homer
Hedgeho

feather

chair

# I i

Where is Dudley going in such a hurry?
He is an impossible driver, isn't he?
He should stop his automobile while looking for "I's."

tiny insect

Ichabod
Fish

*Did you invite HIM?*

ice cream

tire

dish

pie

knife

Indian

pipe

a frightened alligator

*Impossible driver!*

# J j

a jolly
jack-o-lantern

Janitor Joe

pajamas

JENNY

jeep

Just look at the jumble!
Janitor Joe enjoys
jolting journeys
in his pajamas.

# K k

Look! Sam has put on a new disguise.
Now he is a big cake on a bike. Yum-yum!

cake

bike

Kid Kelly
skating to kindergarten

Hi, Kid!

kerchief

Kate Kitty

cook
in back
of truck

fork

KATE'S
BAKERY

NO PARKING

stick

truck

L l

flashing light

Louie,
the policeman

tall lamp

taillight

ladder

POLICE

manhole

Well, see where Dudley landed!
He didn't look where he was going.
He is disguised as three-flavored
ice cream from Tillie's lawn party.
Be careful, Dudley! Children
like to eat delicious ice cream!

GO
LEFT

letter   box

yellow line

letters

a yelling mailman

a little girl

sidewalk

Now...has everyone
found all the "L's" to put
in Sam's sack?

# M m

helmet

motorcycle

hammer

Foolish Fox, the mechanic

mop

broom

Mother Goose

smokestack

locomotive

Mr. Foolish Fox, the mechanic, is
hammering the bumps out of Dudley's car.
Sam has made himself a new disguise to
wear while he looks for "M's."

milk carton

GRADE A MILK

MILK

platform

Mrs. Mouse

# N n

Dudley can't fool anyone in his new disguise.
A lot of people already think he's a nut! But a nice,
lovable, funny sort of nut, of course.
Look out, Dudley! That hungry elephant likes peanuts.

sun

handle

frying pan

signal

nut

hungry elephant's trunk

passenger train

bent nail

conductor

Ned Lion

Nurse
Bella

9

CANDY

SANDWICHES

NO
SNORING
IN THE
STATION

hand car

newsboy

trunk

Oscar Crow

O swald O wl

O O

so ldier

o ld cann o n

fo rt

Ole Octopus is rowing his old, hole-y rowboat out to the queen's palace. His two funny-looking passengers seem to be on the lookout for "O's."

O le O cto pus

a round o range

a c o il of r o pe

r o wb o at

b o tt o m of the o cean

The round orange on the rowboat shouts, "I can see four 'O's' in 'the bottom of the ocean,' Dudley."

# P p

pennant

palace

The people at the palace are very pleased to see the passengers on the rowboat. Papa Peter has made a platter of slippery spaghetti for them.

spaghetti

Papa Peter

TO PAPA PETERS PIZZA PARLOR

portal

steps

purple paint

painter

Squire Quigley

quiver

# Q q

The queen is quaffing a quart of quince juice.

1 Quart

The Squirming Quartet

quay

As they quit the quay, the queen quickly asks a question: "Have you all been minding your 'P's' and your 'Q's'? Have you?"

# Rr

What is the best disguise to wear at an airport? An airplane disguise, of course! There are so many airplanes here that nobody will ever discover Dudley searching for "R's."

control tower

rad

Captain Roger

engineer

first officer

RANDOM AIRPORT

REST ROO

waiting room

stewardess

four furious crew members

helicopter

parachute

crash landing

SWISSAIR

front door

rear door

ground crewman

aviator

stairs

# S s

searchlight

sailplane

GAS

striped stand

SALLY'S SANDWICH SHOP

spiral descent

grass

customers swallowing sandwiches

passenger bus

scrubber

Sam has been trying to *fly* his disguise. But Sam's disguise just doesn't fly so well.

soap suds

SAM'S SACK

STOP

safety sign

*Hi, Sid!*

*Hi, Saul!*

Now put all your letters in Sam's sack, please.

soaked mouse

**T t**

tree

TOM TAILOR

TED BUTCHER

TINA'S TOYS

tomato

Sergeant Murphy

STOP!

meat

hydrant

traffic light

Two turtles are traveling through the tiny town. Look! Their little car has hit a little tomato cart. *SPLAT!* Twenty-two thousand tomatoes have been spilt!

dent

cart

Tom Tiger

TELEPHONE

Neat Timothy, the street cleaner, has fainted.

telephone booth

# U u

umbrella

Uncle Louie

underwear

HOUSE OF MUSIC

SUBWAY

UNIFORMS

nurse

Uncle Louie jumped up in the air.
But his suit stayed behind.
Can you find any "T's" and "U's"
under all those tomatoes?

Uriah Duck
ducking

dump truck

blue suit

mud

curb

# V v

violin

vase

shovel

*V-a-r-o-o-m!* Have you ever seen such driving?
NO! Never, ever!

VINNY and VIKKI MOVERS
"WE LOVE TO MOVE"

Vinny, the driver

lovely Virginia's violent vacuum cleaner

vine

violets

clover

five leaves

CURVE

Victor Dove

river

gravy boat

# W w

woods

Willy Wolf, the witty woodchopper, is working along the wayside.
Suddenly he whistles wildly.
"Well," he says, "I have seen cars drive in the woods, but I have never seen woods drive in a car."

Wilbur Crow

strawberries

yellow vest

Walter Walrus wearing a watch at his wrist

wood

Haw! Haw! Haw!

wheel

two wrestlers

GO SLOW

# X x

Max Ox doesn't exactly watch where he is going. He needs to have his eyes examined.

six boxes of eggs

EXTRA FRESH EGGS

EXIT

Max Ox

EXPRESS

TAXI

exquisite Miss Trixi

X CROSS ROADS

Xavier Lynx

ax

Foolish Fox

*Excuse me!*

# Y y

hydrant

ONE WAY

Yikes!

Yvonne Kitty

Harry Hyena

Yum! Yum!

yellow yolk

frying pan

Harry Hyena is very hungry.
Why is he suddenly so happy?

# Z z

SAM'S SACK

zebra

Sam's pants,
unzipped

zipper

Zip,
the postman

Izzy and
Zelda Lizard

Bugdozer

At last we have come to the last
letter of the alphabet—"Z."
Find the "Z's" and finish putting
your letters in Sam's sack.
   Just a minute! Sam's pants
are unzipped. Zip up your pants,
Sam, so you can walk.

Aa Bb Cc Dd

Gg Hh Ii Jj

Mm Nn Oo Pp

Rr Ss Tt Uu

Ww Xx Yy Zz

" 'ey, 'arry! You're dropping your 'H's'!"
"I know, 'enry.
I can't 'elp it.
It's a bad 'abit I 'ave!"

hHHh H h H HHhH

# Ee Ff

# Kk Ll

# Qq

# Vv

Ah! There is Lowly Worm painting
all the letters of the alphabet.
And what are Sam and Dudley doing
with all the letters we have found?
They are making an *alphabet soup!*
That's what they are doing.
Stanley is slowly stirring the soup.
Mmmmmm! It does smell good.

Now…let's all sit down and eat it.

Say!!! Who put the shoe
in the alphabet soup?
*That's* not a shoe!
That's Lowly Worm in disguise.
All right, Mister Shoe—
please get out of the soup.
You're not a letter of the alphabet!

SOUP
SERVER
PATENT
APPLIED FOR